MW00965481

Duo for
Obstinate Voices

Maryse Pelletier

Duo for
Obstinate Voices

A play
translated by
Louise Ringuet

Guernica

Original Title:
Duo pour voix obstinées.
Copyright © 1985 by VLB Éditeur and Maryse Pelletier.
Translation © 1990 by Louise Ringuet and Guernica Editions.

Guernica Editions gratefully acknowledge financial support
from the Canada Council and Le ministère des Affaires culturelles.

Antonio D'Alfonso
Guernica Editions, P.O. Box 633, Station N.D.G.,
Montreal (Quebec), Canada H4A 3R1
Legal Deposit — Fourth Quarter
Bibliothèque nationale du Québec & National Library of Canada.

Canadian Cataloguing in Publication Data

Pelletier, Maryse
(Duo pour voix obstinées. English)
Duo for obstinate voices

(Drama series; 3)
Translation of: Duo pour voix obstinées.
ISBN 0-920717-17-9 (bound). —
ISBN 0-920717-16-0 (pbk.)

I. Title. II. Title: Duo pour voix obstinées. English. III. Series.

PS8581.E39875D9313 1990   C842'.54   C88-090069-5
PQ3919.2.P44D9313 1990

Note

This play sprang from me with the force of a river breaking through a dam. I laid a few dikes and let the flow run its course. I had no choice. I kept hearing a symphony of colors, a thundering flood of sensations. But mostly, I kept hearing a voice, coming from deep down, an obstinate, relentless, stubborn voice which kept saying: Why? Why? Why so many crumbled dreams? Why this constant need to feel good, to possess, to hurt, to be hurt? Why do we crave for love, for hate? Why?

The play has been written and the same obstinate voice is still there fiercely asking: Why? Only less often now. There is another voice, just as stubborn, which from time to time says: This is how it is, this is how it is, that is all.

Duo for Obstinate Voices takes place in Quebec between 1970 and 1975, a period marked by the emergence of a strong nationalist movement which led to the election in 1976 of the Parti Québécois which made the independence of Quebec the cornerstone of its political program. The rest is history.

It is also history that from 1970 onwards many journalists, like a large number of the young intellectuals, supported the Parti Québécois. Journalists, within the bounds of their professional ethics, gave the independence movement a political forum and, in doing so, responded to the wishes of an increasing number of persons. The attitude of the protagonist, Philip, is therefore far from surprising.

I never explicitly mention Quebec's vision of independence because it is my belief that all groups, all nations have dreams which human beings naturally carry with them. Many in the audience, in whatever country the play be produced, are likely to recognize in Philip's dream their own or that of their countrymen. And this is my dearest dream.

With special thanks to François, Gilbert, Paul, Hélène, Gilles and to everyone who, in one way or another, contributed to bringing this play into existence.

Maryse Pelletier

Duo pour voix obstinées was first performed at Théâtre d'Aujourd'hui in Montreal, Quebec, on January 17, 1985, with the following cast: Hélène Mercier, Paul Savoie and Gilles Michaud. The play was directed by François Barbeau. The costumes were designed by Jean-Yves Cadieux; the set by André Hénault and the lighting by Jocelyn Proulx. The original music was composed by François Trudeau.

Duo for Obstinate Voices was presented as a public reading at Playwrights' Workshop Montreal on September 29, 1986 and was directed by Michael Springate. The three actors who lent their voices to the characters were Mark Walker, Jeannie Walker and Vittorio Rossi.

The Characters

PHILIP. A handsome, charming, nervous, voluble and enterprising man, self-aware, and conscious of his image. A television journalist. Thirty-three years old at the beginning, he is 38 at the end of the play.

CATHRYN. A beautiful young woman who, at the beginning of the play, displays a somewhat gloomy disposition but, as the play progresses, opens up. Sensitive, sharp, entirely focused on her inner life. Her ambition is to become a dancer. Twenty-three years old at the beginning of the play, she is 28 at the end.

VALENTINO. An Italian waiter, who emigrated to Quebec only a few years before the play begins. A modest man, open, charming, talkative. He is in his late twenties when the story begins and five years older at the end. During the course of the play, he gradually loses his Italian accent.

SCENE ONE

ALLEGRO MA NON TROPPO

Ignorance

Philip enters. He is a handsome man of almost forty years old. He seems bitter and tries to justify himself. He addresses the audience.

PHILIP

I do not care what anybody says. I have worked hard! Non-stop! Sure I had talent, but I still had to work. Eighteen years I have been a journalist. And in those eighteen years I have seen just about everything and done just about as much. But no! That doesn't count! Who knows what counts around here. Jesus, I almost got killed once doing a documentary! This bullet went right through the headrest.

And would have gone right through my head if I hadn't happened to bend down! Which goes to show you how little we matter. Anyway, if I had been killed, it wouldn't have mattered one bit. Nothing matters around here for more than two days. If we had really wanted the revolution to succeed, we would have had to wrap the whole thing up in two days. You want to have impact, you have to live your whole life in two days. It is totally absurd!

Philip joins Cathryn who is sitting at a table in a small Italian restaurant. He is in his early thirties, proud, charming, seductive and in good spirits. Cathryn hangs on his every word. They are about to have coffee. The table has almost been completely cleared. Although they have had a few drinks, they are not drunk.

Background music of the type one usually hears in Italian restaurants. Philip has to break up the pleasant, conventional, subdued atmosphere.

PHILIP

With an Italian accent.

Valentino!

VALENTINO

Moving toward the table.

Sir?

PHILIP

Bring us some champagne, Valentino! I promise we will leave soon but first we want the best champagne in the house.

CATHRYN

Yes, Valentino, champagne! Champagne and then we will be off, stumbling all the way, perhaps...

VALENTINO

Are you celebrating something?

PHILIP

Oh yes, indeed! I am celebrating my meeting with this wonderful woman, a wonderful city, a fabulous week and fabulous friends! An occasion like this calls for champagne, especially since I have a story to tell Cathryn.

VALENTINO

A story...? Then you need two bottles maybe, no?

PHILIP

You devil, you! You are going to be a rich man one day, that's for sure!

Valentino goes out laughing.

CATHRYN

A true story?

PHILIP

Always!

CATHRYN

With a happy ending?

PHILIP

Always! Especially with champagne!

CATHRYN

Why? Crying is not permitted while drinking champagne?

PHILIP

Never. It is an insult to life, an insult to happiness.

CATHRYN

Why? I would prefer a story that's half-jolly, half-glum.

12

PHILIP

Tut tut! Strictly forbidden! I want you bright and positive with that same look in your eyes as when I first saw you.

CATHRYN

That was because I was seeing you for the first time.

PHILIP

At that moment, Cathryn, your eyes were so revealing, I felt I was looking right into your soul.

CATHRYN

Do you know when I realized that you had noticed me? When you asked me to take you around Quebec City! Imagine!

PHILIP

Did you enjoy my documentary?

CATHRYN

Excellent! For once, a documentary that didn't hide dancers' sweat. I mean you could almost smell it!

PHILIP

Worried.

What?

CATHRYN

It is about time people found out what dance is all about!

PHILIP

You are wrong! People want to be told that dancing is beautiful, exciting, fascinating, difficult, anything but that it smells sweaty!

CATHRYN

Somewhat boldly.

Nor, I suppose, that dancers stuff their dance belts so they have a big one?

PHILIP

Prudish.

Cathryn!

CATHRYN

Defending herself.

Oh you never said that, I know.

PHILIP

If that is the impression you got, what is the difference?

CATHRYN

I was simply trying to tell you your documentary was good…

PHILIP

Sure, but you are a dancer. You hardly represent the general public!

Cathryn sits back in her chair.

Valentino brings the bottle of champagne in a bucket. Philip turns rapidly around and greets Valentino with open arms.

PHILIP

Valentino! Thank God, you are not a dancer. You sure know how to serve champagne, though! And serving champagne is an art too!

VALENTINO

Ah, the young lady is a dancer?

PHILIP

Charmingly.

Haven't you noticed the way she walks? Like a feline: sleek, graceful, strong.

CATHRYN

Responding to the compliment.

Come on, most of the time, I stagger along because my muscles ache so much!

PHILIP

Laughing.

Would you look at those legs, Valentino, pure prima ballerina style!

CATHRYN

She tries to hide her legs.

Stop it, I hate my calves!

VALENTINO

You are on TV as well?

CATHRYN

I haven't lowered myself to that yet.

PHILIP

See, my friend, how this younger generation looks down on us. I am telling you, they're against success.

CATHRYN

I am only against what you have to do to get there, it isn't really the same thing!

PHILIP

That is exactly what I mean. They are against talent! You see that?

CATHRYN

Not in a million years!

PHILIP

Well, I hope you kids have nothing against champagne at least. Do you?

CATHRYN

Come on, I'm only against backstabbing and bootlicking, or should I say ballet shoe licking. I mean, I might be against wheeling and dealing just to get up there, but I am *for* champagne!

PHILIP

He raises his glass.

To your blossoming talent, my dear!

CATHRYN

She raises her glass as well.

17

Mine is only a budding talent; yours is in full bloom!

PHILIP

Why don't you join us, Valentino?

VALENTINO

He helps himself.

Thank you, Sir!

PHILIP

So, when do you plan to move to Montreal?

VALENTINO

I don't know… in time… I don't know when.

He pours himself a drink.

For the moment, let's drink to your future.

PHILIP

To yours, Valentino!

VALENTINO

To yours, Miss!

They drink.

Short pause.

CATHRYN

Ah, the future, the future! Come on, Philip, play the fortune teller, what is it going to be?

PHILIP

For Valentino: an Italian restaurant, the biggest and best in Montreal. And for you: it will be the day that you dance on points and join one of the biggest dance companies in the world!

CATHRYN

That is a long way off, even for the points! But I wasn't talking in a professional sense, I'm sorry. So, what about that story?

To Valentino.

He said he had a story to tell me.

To Philip.

Come on!

PHILIP

Don't worry, Valentino, we won't be long.

VALENTINO

No problem. I never heard you tell a short story before, Mister Philip. Take all the time you need. I am in no hurry!

Lighting change. Valentino addresses the audience. He is all charm, sure of himself, cheerful.

L'amore, l'amore! There is nothing like it. Me, I love the women, all the women. But I don't like when it gets too complicated. *Mamma mia*, when it gets that way, I am gone! I don't understand that stuff in the papers, some people they go crazy, they kill and strangle for love. Love is simple. When it is finished, you leave, and that is it! *(L'amore è semplice. Quando è finito, te ne vai. Tutto qua!)*

Exit Valentino.

Lights on Philip and Cathryn

PHILIP

The story that I want to tell is *my* story…

CATHRYN

Hm…!

PHILIP

…Which happens to be the story of a nation.

CATHRYN

Do it as if you were doing a newscast, ok?

20

PHILIP

Playing the newscaster each time he tells his story, at any case for the beginning moments.

Okay... Good evening, Ladies and Gentlemen...

CATHRYN

Laughing.

Good!

PHILIP

Tonight, I will take you into the heart of a land, an unknown land, where wheat grows...

CATHRYN

Wanting to participate.

...In the middle of stony fields...

PHILIP

What? Where?

CATHRYN

Back home, in the Gaspé, that's how it is. One weed, one stone; one weed, one stone...

PHILIP

You are kidding? Well then, bring the Gaspé along, it is part of the country too!

CATHRYN

All right, let's go!

PHILIP

...Ladies and Gentlemen, let me take you to a land, as yet unknown or rather, undiscovered — where wheat grows, sometimes in the middle of stony fields — a new country, a young country just becoming conscious of its own existence, bordered on the north by a multitude of virgin rivers which have been flowing from time immemorial, rivers which will soon be harnessed so that their clear, cold water can provide a whole continent with energy...

CATHRYN

Wow!

PHILIP

In one breath.

...A country whose southern border is sinking into thick mud, black and rich mud born out of money and sweat...

CATHRYN

It must be hard to dance with lead boots on!

PHILIP

When you are into making money, you don't think about dancing, you can be sure of that.

CATHRYN

Sullenly.

I know, dance is pretty insignificant compared to the rest.

PHILIP

No, it isn't. Look at this younger generation. They give up even before they start!

CATHRYN

I am sorry. I think I said that because I feel a little sad, that is all. It is the image of the mud.

PHILIP

When you want to succeed in life, sweetheart, sadness is a waste of time.

He fills her glass.

CATHRYN

She moves forward in her chair.

Especially with champagne! Go on with your story, I won't interrupt anymore.

PHILIP

Look at me, I'm living through a nightmare: a divorce. Now, that is a real nightmare! And I am more active than ever, I believe in things now more than I ever did, and I'm much older than you!

CATHRYN

Ten years! It isn't much. Besides, keeping busy must help you forget.

PHILIP

I am not in this line of work to forget, it would be ludicrous. It would be like doing away with my soul.

CATHRYN

I know, I know. Go on with your story!

PHILIP

With a new surge of energy.

...So, in that country, lived a people who had developed rounded backs from constantly gazing at their navels, a bald headed, bent over population, a pious population which had lost its soul, which had smothered its soul, I should say — and suddenly, there was a tremor — like the first tremor going through a beast about to awaken. And then there were bombs! Isn't it marvelous?

CATHRYN

Scandalized.

You call that marvelous?

PHILIP

Come on, Cathryn, you have to look beyond lawfulness, beyond morality. Do you know what our real morals are? Do you? It is asking the priest: "Father, is fucking a sin?" And he answers: "Yes, if you do it from the front but, no, if you do it from the back" ...or should it be the other way around? This is the kind of morals we have! Wonderful morals, aren't they? Only I never let stuff like that get in my way. That is why I was always able to see what was really happening.

CATHRYN

What do you mean?

PHILIP

Talent is more than being able to see the present facts, it's also being able to see the major trends of the future. And that kind of talent, I had! And still do! You want to hear what I found out today?

CATHRYN

What?

PHILIP

Get ready for this. Starting next week, I am going to be a foreign correspondent. Do you realize what that means?

CATHRYN

Suddenly panicking.

What? You are going to be leaving Montreal?

PHILIP

Of course not! I will be traveling back and forth: two weeks here, three weeks there. This is not what really matters. Foreign correspondent is the summit of a career, the summit of my career, do you understand? It is only fair when you consider how they tried to get rid of me.

CATHRYN

Are you serious?

PHILIP

I swear! They had me doing just about anything. Imagine: the avant-garde dance scene
in Quebec City! They might as well have sent
me to the desert. A good thing you were there!

CATHRYN

So, I was the oasis, eh?

PHILIP

You are really the most interesting person I
have met here, Cathryn!

CATHRYN

Well, thank you.

PHILIP

No, they haven't succeeded in getting rid of
me! I have always gambled on the future. Always saw what was coming. And now, they
have to recognize that I was right and they
have got to make room for me. This is what I
have been dreaming of for twelve years,
Cathryn. This is what I have been struggling
for during the past twelve years! A man isn't a
man until he has the right to build a future for

himself and for the world, at the same time. Do you understand? And today, at last, I can start to do just that! Would you believe it? I now have the right to build, the right to be who I am, the right to live a normal life, the right to fall in love even! I feel like I was twenty again. That is not true, I feel better now than I did at twenty.

CATHRYN

It is a wonderful story!

PHILIP

I had predicted that there would be a tremor! You will see, things will begin to change around here. There will be tremendous, majestic, irresistible changes. And even when I am elsewhere in the world, I will still be part of it. I am in the forefront of that great march. Cathryn, you just don't know how happy I am!

CATHRYN

I am glad for you, Phil, I really am!

Enter Valentino.

PHILIP

My dear Valentino, are you losing your patience?

VALENTINO

No, no, Sir.

PHILIP

This is one of the most important evenings of my life, did you know that?

VALENTINO

Are you getting married, Mister Philip?

PHILIP

Laughing.

No, better than that. I have decided to keep on living. Bring us a last bottle and join us. Please.

VALENTINO

No, no, thank you. I don't want to take you away from the young lady!

PHILIP

Nonsense. She is inviting you. Aren't you, Cathryn?

CATHRYN

Hesitant.

Yes, of course.

VALENTINO

If the young lady says so.

Exit Valentino.

Change of lighting. Spotlight on Cathryn. She rises and addresses the audience.

CATHRYN

When I met Philip, he had a dog. I didn't know anything about dogs then, so I used to stand back. I watched carefully. When two dogs meet, the first thing they do is smell each other. Then, they fight for territory. The one that gives in is saying that the other one is superior; otherwise, they fight to death. And if they are equally strong, then both die. This is the way dogs behave.

Cathryn goes back.

She tries to get Philip on his feet.

CATHRYN

Come and dance with me.

PHILIP

Uncomfortable.

Come on, Cathryn, we are in a restaurant.

CATHRYN

It doesn't matter. There is no one around but the two of us!

PHILIP

I am not a dancer like you, you know that.

CATHRYN

So what. I just want to be close to you, in your arms. Please, this is the last time we are together.

PHILIP

Rising.

Try to understand, Cathryn.

CATHRYN

What, because of Valentino?

PHILIP

Valentino?

CATHRYN

Well, you invited him.

PHILIP

Yes, so?

CATHRYN

I wish we could have been alone for a while longer, just the two of us. But, it's okay, it doesn't matter.

PHILIP

I am a man of action, Cathryn, not a dreamer. I have to move, talk, do things. I don't feel good unless there are people around me.

She puts her arms around him and forces him to move to the music.

CATHRYN

I understand.

Philip lets himself be carried along, his mind however is elsewhere. He gradually loosens up and begins to caress Cathryn tenderly, firmly.

PHILIP

It is unbelievable how firm and supple you are.

CATHRYN

You too.

PHILIP

What are you going to do?

CATHRYN

She shrugs her shoulders.

I don't know. I will see.

PHILIP

Are you going back to your boyfriend's?

CATHRYN

I broke up with him yesterday.

PHILIP

I am sorry, Cathryn. I didn't expect to upset your life like that.

CATHRYN

Shrugging her shoulders.

You haven't. I was going to do it anyway. It just made things happen a little faster. What about you?

PHILIP

Yes? What about me?

33

CATHRYN

Well, you are beginning a new life...

PHILIP

He abruptly stops dancing.

Look, Cathryn, I don't know how to say this, my life is not simple. I am in the process of moving. The kids are with me on weekends. And every second I take for myself makes me feel as if I were stealing that time from my home, my children, my work, my friends... But, if you want to...

CATHRYN

Yes?

PHILIP

Look, I don't want to impose anything on you. You have to watch out for me, Cathy. Most of all, don't ever give up your career. I have been known to ruin people's lives, you know. That is what my wife used to tell me...

CATHRYN

Maybe your wife wasn't strong enough.

PHILIP

Maybe so, but it isn't that simple. You are right in a way. You amaze me, do you know

34

that? You are so young, yet so wise — in any case, it is only if you want to...

CATHRYN

If I want to...?

Enter Valentino.

Philip, uncomfortable, moves away from Cathryn and goes to greet Valentino eagerly.

PHILIP

Valentino! Come and have a drink with us. Excuse me, this is the first time in my life I have ever danced in a restaurant. Young women today have this need to express themselves, you know. They believe in body language. Take my advice, Valentino, don't fall into the trap.

VALENTINO

No more chances for me. I am getting married next Saturday.

PHILIP

You are getting married? What, the tuxedo, the bouquet, the bride all dressed in white, blushing under her veil and the whole she-bang?

VALENTINO

Sì, sì. In church! Like she wanted. Everything is ready. *(È cosi. Tutto è pronto.)*

PHILIP

And I thought that Valentinos were men who had passionate love affairs, who had plenty of young, beautiful, rich mistresses and broke many hearts along the way... So, you're about to settle down and become a stay-at-home bird. Before I know it, you'll close your restaurant at eleven o'clock and I won't be able to come for a late supper anymore.

VALENTINO

No, no. We will stay open. My wife will understand, I swear to you, she will!

PHILIP

Of course, Valentino, of course. I was only kidding. Well, here is to a very happy marriage!

> *They drink, except for Cathryn.*
> *Philip turns around in her direction.*

PHILIP

Aren't you going to drink?

CATHRYN

If I want what, Philip?

PHILIP

Wait a minute.

CATHRYN

Come on, please tell me. I can't stand it anymore. If I want what...? You don't want to see
me anymore, is that it?

PHILIP

What are you saying? I don't want to lose you,
sweetheart. I wouldn't stand losing you. I
want to be able to see you as often as I can. I
don't know how we can manage that, but we
will try. What do you say...?

CATHRYN

*She begins to weep, throwing herself in
Philip's arms.*

Yes. Yes, of course.

PHILIP

On one condition.

CATHRYN

Which one?

PHILIP

Promise me you will never cry again while we are having champagne.

As the set changes, Cathryn steps forward and addresses the audience.

CATHRYN

I often dreamed that I was trying to dance or trying to scream. Dancing or screaming, it is the same thing, really. Even talking in a way. But I could never do it. No more than I could stretch out my arm to the end of my fingers towards my partner.

She extends her arm halfway, for a moment contains her anger, finally pulls back her arm.

The sounds would always get stuck in my throat as if I were choking. I felt so desperate! I would have given my whole life to be able to do things without so much effort, to finally dance without holding back or to cry without holding back and just stand naked in a crowd, naked in front of the whole world. I used to tell myself, it is because I started too late. But that wasn't the reason. I just kept going blindly, trying so hard to stretch out that I kept shrinking. And that used to make me furious. It seemed to me that if I could ever

38

break through that, I would finally be happy.
I would be able to move on to something else.

She turns around and walks back to Philip.

Fade out.

SCENE TWO

ANDANTE CON BRIO

Fear

A year later.

A bar in the Mirabel airport. The setting is tubular, metallic and cold. There are small tables, and the lighting is cozy.

Room noise. Voices. Announcements of arrivals and departures accompanied by the usual preceding signals. Easy-listening and sentimental background music — Muzak.

Enter Philip and Cathryn. She is sober and perplexed. He is light-hearted, some-what drunk, giving the impression that a great weight is off his mind. Philip holds

Cathryn by the shoulders, half-leaning on her, half-kissing her.

PHILIP

Home at last! God, Montreal is beautiful! America is beautiful, you just don't know how much! Cathy, my dear Cathy, you did the right thing — I am so glad you came to pick me up! You don't know how fed up I am with planes! With movies about plane crashes! With scotches at 37,000 feet! With Eurasian stewardesses! Cathy, I can't believe I am finally home. I feel as if I was still in mid-air.

Philip makes a move to sit at a table. Cathryn tries to hold him back.

CATHRYN

Come on, don't stop at the bar, please!

PHILIP

Why not? Of course I am going to stop at the bar!

CATHRYN

Insistent.

Don't you want to go home and get some rest?

PHILIP

No way! I will rest when I am dead and buried! Right now, I'm on the finish line and will sit my behind right here. Airport bar chairs may not be all that comfortable, but just the same, they are as comfortable as anything you would find in American bars. And that, by the way, is four times better than anywhere else in the world. So, for the moment, I need time to land and take a break.

Philip sits. Enter Valentino. Philip notices him and rises immediately, obviously pleased to see him. He greets him with open arms.

PHILIP

Valentino, Valentino, my friend! What are you doing here?

VALENTINO

Happy to see Philip.

Well, Mister Philip, how are you? And it is Miss...? Of course, I remember you, you are the young lady I met last year in Quebec City.

PHILIP

Only goes to show you that I am getting old. And getting attached.

VALENTINO

Well, that is good, real good!

PHILIP

What about you? What has been happening with you, my friend? You moved to Montreal pretty quickly, haven't you?

VALENTINO

My wife wanted to come here, so...

PHILIP

I see! Don't tell me you don't cook anymore? You haven't opened your restaurant yet?

VALENTINO

No, I am saving my money. You see, I am making good money here. I will get my own restaurant faster this way.

PHILIP

To Cathryn.

And then he will get his whole family to come over, watch and see. This is how Italians get their own little family Mafia and become big bosses themselves.

VALENTINO

Oh no, Sir, no need for the Mafia, not since I am here!

PHILIP

Well, aren't you something! You have really adopted Quebec, Valentino, haven't you? Can't say I blame you! Listen, would you bring me a double scotch, please.

VALENTINO

Of course, Sir. What about the young lady, what will she have?

CATHRYN

A gin and tonic, please. A single!

VALENTINO

I will be right back.

> *Valentino is about to leave. Philip stops him and rises.*

PHILIP

> *As if giving a speech that is partially directed to Valentino, partially directed to Cathryn.*

Wait, Valentino, I need a friend by my side. Please, I need a witness, wait. There is something I have been wanting to do ever since I boarded that damn plane.

He points to Cathryn.

You see this woman, Valentino, this child-woman, this irresistible flower in bloom, this image of stubbornness, of fragility, of softness, this unconscious ironlike strength, these delicate wrists and impenetrable eyes, the soft-spoken tenderness and screaming silence, this intelligence and these legs, Valentino, these legs, would you look at this woman, Valentino.

CATHRYN

Philip, please.

PHILIP

Don't you know, Valentino, I thought about her during the whole trip! The whole damn trip! And, believe me, Vietnam is a long way from here, a long way!

VALENTINO

I understand very well.

CATHRYN

Insistent.

Not here, Philip, please.

45

PHILIP

You see, she says that she wants me to keep quiet, but it's not true. Believe me, Valentino, this woman loves me like nobody ever did before, nobody! I can tell her anything, she always understands. She sleeps with me, she never stops thinking about me, she devours me, body and soul, she feeds me, body and soul, and she wants to marry me.

CATHRYN

I never said that.

PHILIP

Well, in front of you, Valentino, is the woman I am proposing to because I have a sudden and irresistible urge to live. I would have loved to bring you back some flowers, Cathryn. If only I was returning from Paris, I could have brought you a few lilies of the valley. And I wouldn't have had to say a single word, you would have understood right away. Instead, all I am left with, Valentino, is the wish for that damn bouquet. Look, I am even getting down on my knees.

He goes on his knees.

I am asking her to share my hopeless life and to bear with my hopeless disposition. I am begging her to be my port in the storm, my continuity, my support and I will be yours, Cathryn. I swear, I won't change my mind and I will remain faithful for as long as you want us to be together. So there! If someone were to kill you here and now, in my arms like this, I would scream from the top of my lungs: "You have taken my life." We are beautiful people you and I, Cathy, so let's love each other and live together? Do say yes.

CATHRYN

Get on your feet, Phil, please. People are looking at us.

PHILIP

Come on, Cathryn, say yes. I feel silly on this dirty rug.

CATHRYN

(*She laughs.*) You are right. You do look a bit silly.

PHILIP

God, I love your laugh, Cathryn! As long as I can make you laugh, we will be happy together. If my being silly makes you laugh, then I will be silly as often as I can. But not for long stretches of time, if you don't mind?

He laughs as well, gets to his feet.

Valentino, you have just witnessed a marriage proposal. The second one I have made so far but, without a doubt, the best one. Bring us something to drink so we can recover from all this emotion.

Valentino leaves. A short pause. Cathryn bursts out laughing.

PHILIP

Do you think it is funny? Isn't that what we wanted? Where our relationship was headed for?

CATHRYN

Before you left, you didn't want to see me anymore. Now, you want to marry me. I don't understand. I swear, I don't.

PHILIP

You must not pay too much attention to my change of moods. Look, sweetheart, I deal with the whole world. I have just returned from Vietnam. I almost got killed twice... You will have to trust me a little and learn to disregard minor details.

CATHRYN

Minor details! You call that minor details?

PHILIP

Have I ever mistreated you? Have I ever cheated on you?

CATHRYN

I don't know.

PHILIP

You don't know? My God, every woman I see reminds me of you. Nothing else in the world matters, believe me. You have to grow up, Cathy, grow up. On certain issues, you are still a little girl.

CATHRYN

On certain issues, I don't think I want to grow up.

PHILIP

Take my house. Turn it upside down, if you wish. Believe me, you will never find a man to be at your beck and call like I will. Seriously, this is what I have been waiting for. Let's make that place our own. When the kids come over, I will make sure they don't disturb us. Let's develop habits, like having tea together at the end of the afternoons. I swear, that is one thing I have always wanted to do. Boy, those British know how to live! Cathryn, let's give ourselves a home where we can simply be ourselves and forget about life's battles. With me, you can be yourself -100%- if you want. All you have to do is say yes.

Spotlight on Philip. He continues his earlier monologue.

PHILIP

It is very interesting to follow politicians, very interesting indeed! They go from one big never-ending discussion to the next, from one dinner reception to the next, from one glass of wine to the next, from one chrysanthemum to the next. But they have no power. Zilch! Zero! It is the paper shufflers, the rats, who wield the real power. Real power is when you can say *no* two days in a row and fight doggedly so as to say *no* one more day and *win*. The rats always win. My God, didn't we have a clear vision of things then? It was so simple. A clear, collective, honest project shining brightly in the sun. Which looks like it could still work. We should not get our hopes up too quickly. The rats are going to gnaw at them. Give them a little time. Rats gnaw everything away: ideas and the people who bear those ideas. A man should go on hiding his visions.

It is the only way he can avoid being hurt.

Back to regular lighting.

Enter Valentino with two glasses.

VALENTINO

Is the contract signed?

PHILIP

Ah, Valentino, these young women of today. They are tougher negotiators than us!

VALENTINO

She only says *no, Sir*, so you should insist a little more. My wife did the same thing.

PHILIP

And you let yourself be trapped into that, a good-looking man like you?

VALENTINO

Oh, I was in love. I didn't mind insisting.

He serves.

I have made everything double, and it's on me.

CATHRYN

Disheartened.

Oh no...

PHILIP

Thank you. I will accept this time, but remember, Valentino, that everytime you do this, you postpone the day you will have your own restaurant.

VALENTINO

Maybe, but what good is a restaurant if the customers are not happy?

PHILIP

You are right. That kind of restaurant never lasts.

VALENTINO

That is what I mean.

Exit Valentino.

Short pause.

CATHRYN

She turns to Philip, blurts out.

I started teaching this week.

PHILIP

Teaching what?

CATHRYN

Dance, of course. To children.

PHILIP

You are wasting your time, Cathryn.

CATHRYN

I have to earn a living, you know.

PHILIP

You should be practicing your point work.

CATHRYN

I will never dance on points. Why even bother thinking about it? My ankles are too weak. All my teachers told me.

PHILIP

Excuses! Excuses!

CATHRYN

And I started taking jazz classes. At least that, I will be able to do.

PHILIP

...What is more, you should be performing.

CATHRYN

It is I who am the dancer, Philip, not you.

PHILIP

You want to *become* a dancer, that is quite different!

CATHRYN

No, it is not.

PHILIP

Yes, it *is* different! Don't get me started on that.

CATHRYN

Sometimes, I wonder if you really want me to be a dancer. If you don't, you should say so right now.

PHILIP

But I do, I do! Sometimes I think I want it even more than you do!

CATHRYN

Ah, come on!

PHILIP

I have told you a million times, you can do anything you want. And what is more, you can take me and do anything with me!

CATHRYN

Sullenly.

Looking after myself is enough for me, thank you.

The lighting changes. Cathryn turns to the audience.

CATHRYN

Puppies are so funny. They all sleep together in a little bunch: back to back, belly to belly, one on top of the other, ass over paws. They are so trusting, so confident! Human beings should be able to sleep like that, it seems to me.

Back to regular lighting.

PHILIP

Coming up with a new idea.

Cathy, we have to arm ourselves with a lot of patience.

CATHRYN

She refuses to follow.

Before I become an accomplished dancer?

PHILIP

No. We have to stock up for a long state of siege. Changes are coming. I know, but they come at a snail's pace around here. We might as well do everything we can to be happy in the meantime.

CATHRYN

Irritated.

Fine with me. As long as you let me speak up once in a while.

PHILIP

You will be able to say anything that is on your mind. You will see how I don't rattle on when I feel good. What I am offering you is a home you can come back to after you have gone out to conquer the world, a shelter where you can withdraw when you're in pain, a haven of peace. Say yes, Cathy, please do. We could even get married. You decide.

CATHRYN

She gives in slowly.

We will see more of each other if we live together?

PHILIP

He moves gently towards her.

We will see each other every night. I want to be able to hold you in my arms every night. I will take you on my trips as often as you can get away. I miss you so much when I go away... Yes?

Cathryn nods yes. Philip is exultant and takes her in his arms and draws her to him.

Life in America is so wonderful and simple!

CATHRYN

How is that?

PHILIP

We're getting married.

CATHRYN

Not quite!

PHILIP

Same thing and I don't need to go courting you at your parents' for three years. I don't have to buy you with a herd of cows or goats.

CATHRYN

Or buffaloes!

Philip speaks with growing passion till the end of the scene; he is deeply moved. Cathryn listens, is moved as well.

PHILIP

Everything is so open and young here! Here, you have a pile of lawnmowers, huge cars, private swimming pools. You have hundreds of sports fanatics drowning in beer and money. You have thousands of businessmen choking up in self-satisfaction while they watch their shares go up on the stock exchange. You have millions of fake cowboys sitting in front of their TV sets, their balls like guns loaded with blank cartridges. They are ready to shoot at anything as long as it moves. Just like their TV heroes. They think they are irresistibly charming, so they do little coochie-coochie coos to their kids, their wives, their mistresses. They spend billions on the construction of highways, which only last three years, and on buildings you can only look at

— not live in — because they forgot to make windows to let in fresh air. They are so pure they don't even masturbate, so clean they smell like stale soap, so stupid they missed the Messiah and are still waiting for him and, every four years, they believe they have elected one. America is everything and anything you want it to be. One day however it will blow up like a fat toad that little boys are forcing to smoke a cigarette. Yet it remains the only place in the world where you have the right to have kids because it is the only place in the world where they still have a chance not to be scalded at birth, or tortured or starved or crushed to death.

Philip and Cathryn exit.

Fade out.

SCENE THREE

STACCATO

Domination

A year later.

*The dining room of a wealthy house.
The set is elaborate: paintings, sophisticated lighting.*

Evening. Cathryn wears a leotard. She stretches her arms and legs to and fro, practices the movements for the show to be held the following day. She is nervous, resembles a taut spring on the verge of sudden release.

Philip sits at the end of the table — a half-empty glass of wine and a plate before him — silently finishing his meal.

Obviously bored and tense, he abruptly pushes the plate aside.

CATHRYN

What is the matter?

PHILIP

I don't like eating by myself.

CATHRYN

Trying to be helpful, nice.

I am sorry, Phil. I couldn't wait for you. I can't go to sleep on a full stomach, you know. Especially not tonight. Do you want some more wine?

PHILIP

Sure. What about you?

CATHRYN

No, but I'll get you some if you want.

PHILIP

I hate drinking by myself as much as I hate eating by myself.

CATHRYN

Oh stop it. Look, at least I am here. Touch!

She presents him her rear end. He touches her with the tip of his finger.

PHILIP

You present yourself from the rear now? That's something new.

CATHRYN

It just happened that way. Look, I will turn around if you want!

Executes a pirouette and a movement from her choreography. Then, facing him, she looks at him with an engaging smile.

PHILIP

Sarcastic.

Is this from your choreography? Nice!

CATHRYN

Ignoring the sarcasm.

I guess it doesn't look like much the way I just did it, but when we do it together, the four girls upstage, I am sure it will have an effect. Look again.

She does the movement again, this time with more ease. Philip does not budge.

PHILIP

If it is supposed to have such an effect, you should be doing it downstage, not upstage.

CATHRYN

I don't decide such things.

PHILIP

Don't you ever speak up?

CATHRYN

I will, when the time is right. I am not ready yet. You know what, I taught the other girls a movement I can't even do myself.

PHILIP

What kind of a movement can that be, you mind telling me?

CATHRYN

Well, it isn't really the movement I am having trouble with, it's the sound that goes with it. Look, you tap your foot and you make a sound, a sound that I call a dog sound. Like this.

> *Cathryn taps her foot and simultaneously, in rhythm, makes a sound. The sound gets stuck in her throat and only barely resembles the howling of a dog.*

PHILIP

This is your choreography?

CATHRYN

I know. It isn't right. It sounds more like the
wailing of a cat in heat. It's really supposed to
be a dog practicing sounds. That makes it
much more fun, you see.

PHILIP

How did you manage to teach them something you can't do yourself?

CATHRYN

I recorded Monsignor last summer, remember? There are times when I get it, not every
time, but sometimes I do.

PHILIP

Dogs really impress you, don't they?

CATHRYN

Suddenly on her guard.

I guess.

PHILIP

Well, in any case, you can't say that you
haven't learned a few things from me.

CATHRYN

I would never have thought about saying anything like that. You have taught me a lot of
things. Still do. And now, on that note, I am
going to bed.

*Cathryn gets up and goes towards Philip
to kiss him goodnight.*

PHILIP

Just like that?

CATHRYN

Just like that. One little foot in front of the
other right into the bedroom.

PHILIP

You are leaving me by myself, just like that. I
get home late, I have worked all day, and...

Ironic.

I suppose you didn't watch my newscast, my
wonderful local newscast, did you?

CATHRYN

No, I'm sorry. I didn't. I was rehearsing.

PHILIP

It was my best one of the week.

CATHRYN

I am not surprised, I always miss your best ones.

PHILIP

I come home expecting to see you and you go to bed as soon as I get here.

CATHRYN

It's late for me, you know.

PHILIP

Give me at least five minutes. Don't I deserve that much? Five short little minutes, then I'll let you go.

CATHRYN

Well, all right. Five minutes.

Cathryn sits down.

PHILIP

Are you going to count the minutes?

CATHRYN

Of course, not.

Cathryn stretches her leg.

PHILIP

Can't you stop exercising for five minutes?

CATHRYN

Okay.

Cathryn brings her leg back. She starts massaging the muscles of her inner thighs.

PHILIP

You should drink some wine. It would help you relax.

CATHRYN

I can't, Phil, you know that! What was your newscast about today?

PHILIP

It isn't important. Just the run-of-the-mill. But one of these days, very soon, watch it, I am going to lead some politician into saying the exact opposite of what this other guy from his party said the day before. And, of course, I always end my interviews with a question because I can't draw my own conclusions, you see, since I don't have the right to be intelligent.

CATHRYN

And it works?

PHILIP

Of course it works, otherwise I would not be doing it. I don't have that much time to waste. They have assigned me to the local news to punish me. But that is no reason to let them ruin my career. Hell no! My God, the local scene is boring! Jesus, we're insignificant. And not too quick either. The worst thing is that it might never change. Never! That frightens me. It's always the same church basement performances, the same petty local quarrels, nothing but big speeches by idiots who have no vision, and everybody revels in that bullshit.

CATHRYN

What can I tell you, we are what we are! Well, I am going to bed.

Cathryn rises. Philip stops here.

PHILIP

Have you taken the puppy to get vaccinated yet?

CATHRYN

Massaging her thigh.

No, I was rehearsing all day.

PHILIP

What is wrong with your thighs? Are you hurt?

CATHRYN

I must have pinched a nerve. I am afraid I won't be able to do full stretches tomorrow.

PHILIP

You are always afraid you won't be able to do full stretches.

CATHRYN

You are exaggerating, Phil. I have a performance tomorrow. It isn't the same thing. Will you be coming?

PHILIP

I don't think so. I have to go out of town to cover a story.

CATHRYN

You can't find somebody to replace you?

PHILIP

No, Cathryn. I can't.

CATHRYN

You have gotten replacements before.

PHILIP

Not for a reason like that.

CATHRYN

Then, why don't you come after your news-cast? I don't come on till the end of the show.

PHILIP

It isn't that I don't want to go. I'm afraid I'm going to finish late. Don't be upset with me.

CATHRYN

I'm not. I will give them instructions to let you in, just in case you change your mind.

Changing the subject.

I just realized. We each have a show tomor-row. Funny, isn't it?

PHILIP

Not really!

CATHRYN

She is about to leave again.

… Well, since tomorrow is my first real show, and, since I'm not as experienced as you are, I am more nervous than you are. And it isn't just my brain which will be working, but every muscle of my body. And since I want my show to be at least as good as your worst one…

PHILIP

…You're going to bed!

CATHRYN

You got it!

Cathryn is on her way. Philip holds her back.

PHILIP

Come on, take a little sip of wine first. It will relax you.

CATHRYN

Phil, please don't! You know it isn't good for me.

PHILIP

Insistent and abrupt.

Come on. The state you are in, you are going to toss and turn for a whole hour. Drink a little wine, it will help you sleep.

CATHRYN

All right. But only a sip.

Cathryn goes to pour some wine for herself.

PHILIP

Dancing shouldn't stop you from living.

CATHRYN

It doesn't.

PHILIP

When do you think you will have time to take the puppy to the vet?

CATHRYN

Evasive.

I don't know. Early next week maybe.

PHILIP

Incisive.

You won't go next week anymore than you have this past week.

CATHRYN

I was rehearsing.

PHILIP

So were you last week.

CATHRYN

I have been rehearsing intensively for two months, Philip.

PHILIP

And when you rehearse, you don't have time to live.

CATHRYN

It isn't like this all the time, and you know it.

PHILIP

What is going to happen when your career really takes off?

CATHRYN

I will get used to it. You don't seem to understand, this is my first real show.

PHILIP

You are not sixteen, Cathy. You are twenty-five years old!

CATHRYN

What difference does it make? Being twenty-five doesn't make me less nervous.

PHILIP

Haven't you noticed that the minute you start working you let everything else drop. You suddenly become invisible, absent, elusive. You put me on a back-burner. I can't see you, I can't talk to you.

CATHRYN

It is a question of schedules. We have conflicting schedules.

PHILIP

You could make an effort, say once a week. Is that asking too much? Just so I can catch a glimpse of you and be reminded that we are living together.

CATHRYN

You are exaggerating again, Phil. It isn't that bad. We saw each other yesterday and the day before that, and...

PHILIP

Will you ever learn to relax?

CATHRYN

Starting to lose her patience.

I have a show tomorrow, Philip. A show. Will you please get that into your head?

PHILIP

Show or no show, when will you learn to relax?

CATHRYN

Irritated.

What do you mean: learn to relax?

PHILIP

Do you realize that you never laugh? Never, never, never!

CATHRYN

I never laugh! How's that?

PHILIP

You should have seen yourself at the last party we gave. That I gave!

CATHRYN

I cooked, remember, but I suppose that doesn't count!

PHILIP

You looked so damned unpleasant that I felt like asking everybody to leave after half an hour! It is a good thing my friends are sophisticated enough not to take offense. I know journalists bore you, but you could make an effort not to show it so much, at least not to their faces!

CATHRYN

That's not it. I was tired, and when I'm tired, nothing's funny, nothing's interesting... Why won't you let me go to bed?

PHILIP

Go ahead. Go. I am not stopping you. If you think it is going to make you any better, go to bed. Go!

CATHRYN

Cathryn rises, takes three steps, then turns around.

What do you mean by that?

PHILIP

By what?

CATHRYN

If I think it is going to make me any better?

76

How can you tell whether I am good or not, you have never even seen me dance.

PHILIP

I don't need to see you dance. Do you know what you project?

CATHRYN

No, I don't. What do I project?

PHILIP

Tension. Dryness. You are the embodiment of unhappiness. You don't get one ounce of fun out of life, and yet, you want to dance. In front of an audience, besides. You will never get out of the boring avant-garde, Cathryn, never. You will keep on performing for three or four hundred people, at the most, who are exhilarated at having understood something, when there was absolutely nothing to understand, mind you, or seen something marvelous on a pitch-black stage. Is that what you want? Is this why you have been rehearsing for months, taking classes for years? Every week since I have known you, you either stretch yourself out of proportion, sprain your ankles, dislocate your joints or break down from sheer exhaustion.

CATHRYN

Livid.

I knew it. You don't like my work. You should have said so before.

PHILIP

That is not the point. Not at all.

CATHRYN

Oh yes, it is. Why don't you admit it?

PHILIP

I couldn't care less what you do!

CATHRYN

That is exactly what I mean!

PHILIP

What I want to see you do is learn to live like a human being.

CATHRYN

She finishes her glass of wine and pours another one.

What does learning to live like a human being mean? Going to sleep drunk as a skunk every night, laughing at everybody, everybody that isn't fortunate enough to be one of the gang,

78

that is, finding them ridiculous and stupid simply because they are unable to recite, in one breath, the latest news in the world?

PHILIP

So, that is what you got out of it? You have been living here for a year stretching your arms, your legs, watching what you eat, watching how you sit. Heaven help you if you find an ounce of fat or skin on your body that isn't where it is supposed to be! You watch every word you say, you pose, you look at everything and everybody with disdain, you never express any emotion, nor the least sign of contentment, and yet you have the nerve to criticize the type of work we do. You judge my friends, my life.

CATHRYN

I am not judging anyone, but I have realized one thing. You and your friends constantly talk about the same issue: news, news, news. You all talk at the same time, you all steal scoops from each other, you are all jealous of each other. It might be super interesting for you guys, but for anybody else around you, it is super boring!

PHILIP

You can't stand to see us enjoying ourselves, because you are incapable of it.

CATHRYN

That isn't true.

PHILIP

Oh yes, it is. Why don't you admit, once and for all, that you don't feel good about your work. If you at least enjoyed what you did, it would be an improvement.

CATHRYN

Profoundly hurt, she attacks clumsily.

I may not feel good about my work, like you say, I may not be getting as much fun out of life as you people, but no dog ever died because of me, no one ever died by *my* fault.

Lighting changes. Spotlight on Cathryn. She displays the same emotion, but with softness and anxiety.

CATHRYN

Puppies, at one point, practice sounds. Just for fun. They howl and bark all day long. The mother doesn't fret over it. She encourages them, teaches them new sounds. Babies do the same thing. I don't know why mothers can't tell the difference between babies who cry and babies who are trying out their voices.

Back to regular lighting. The scene continues. Philip also is hurt.

PHILIP

It was not my fault, Cathy. It was an accident.

CATHRYN

Quite angry with him.

You thought it was funny to see Monsignor run in the streets at five o'clock in the morning. You were laughing. Everybody was laughing and that got him all excited. He was wild like a puppy.

PHILIP

It was funny.

CATHRYN

No, it wasn't. It was dangerous. And when the car came along, it was even less funny. Everybody was laughing so hard that it took a while to realize he'd been hit. It was wrong to get him excited, it was wrong to let him out loose, it was wrong!

PHILIP

So why didn't you bring him back if you are so smart?

CATHRYN

It was not my dog, it was yours.

PHILIP

Of course. You only mind what is yours. Your own petty little business. "My legs. My ass. My show." But everything else, you don't pay any attention to, why should you?

CATHRYN

That's not true. That's not true.

She bursts into tears before giving in.

I loved Monsignor, but I was afraid of him. I was afraid. He was too big for me, Phil, I felt like I didn't know him well enough. I was afraid of him, I knew he growled even when he was happy. That dog was alone too much. I knew all that, but it didn't stop me from being afraid. I never could get used to him.

PHILIP

Softly now. He is calmer, encouraging even, somewhat at a loss and protective.

You want a dog of your own? Another one, smaller; you could train it yourself, take it anywhere you would want to. A dog that would be yours, Cathryn?

CATHRYN

Completely defeated.

No, thank you. I don't, no. He would die too.
I can't. I break glasses, plants rot on me, I
can't look after a dog.

PHILIP

Of course, you can. You have to be a little
more careful.

CATHRYN

I will never be a good dancer either, I know it.
It doesn't matter. Give me some wine. It
doesn't really matter anymore.

PHILIP

Don't dramatize things.

CATHRYN

I wish I had been born with the gift of life.
Been a good, fertile soil. But no, I come from
a stony land. The only thing that grows there
are scrubby little trees. I am so tired, but it
doesn't matter anymore.

PHILIP

All I am saying is that you should open up a
little.

CATHRYN

I know and I want to, but it is easier said than done. Why don't you tell me what to do, Phil? Everything you have said is true. It is true: I am living with you and most of the time I am not even conscious of being here. I don't know what goes on around me, half the time... It's awful, but what do you want me to do? I can't just stop everything.

PHILIP

Why don't you finish your wine and come to bed.

CATHRYN

She laughs.

Now? I am ready to stay up all night and you are the one telling me to go to bed!

PHILIP

You are performing tomorrow, Cathy.

CATHRYN

She gets up exhausted, Philip almost supports her. He rubs her back between the shoulder blades.

My back hurts, right between the shoulder blades. How weird! I have never hurt there before. What is going to happen to me tomorrow?

84

She laughs and stops.

I have got a good one for you.

PHILIP

What?

CATHRYN

Wait. You want me to tell you? You are going to love it.

PHILIP

What is it?

CATHRYN

She laughs and cries at the same time, as she throws punches at him.

I thought it was funny when Monsignor was running crazy in the streets. I laughed, just like everybody else. I laughed.

Spotlight on Philip who now addresses the audience. As bitter as before, he continues his earlier monologue.

PHILIP

And yet, I used to have big, big, big visions! I used to see myself in every reporters' gallery of the world. I used to dream of the great statesmen who were the souls of their countries. I dreamed of joint responsibilities linking one country to the next. I wanted to denounce all scandals, from the smallest to the biggest. I imagined I was fighting to expose them, in the name of freedom of the press! Freedom of expression! I have said everything that had to be said, but I never really had to fight. Then I gave up. From one year to the next, I could have just repeated the same news bulletins, all I had to do was change the names and other details. I wonder if freedom of expression is any good if it doesn't allow you to move forward? My father killed himself out of sadness because he had failed in everything. I have succeeded in everything, but it hasn't changed a single thing. So what am I supposed to do?

Fade out.

SCENE FOUR

ADAGIO SOSTENUTO

Possession

One year later. Same apartment as in Scene 3. The dining room.

Background music: Mozart or Beethoven.

Cathryn sits at the table, wearing a comfortable nightgown and woolen socks, no shoes. She is knitting. Philip, in the bedroom, whistles as he packs his clothes in a suitcase.

At the beginning of the scene, Cathryn is lost in her thoughts, her knitting resting on her knees. Philip's whistling grows louder. Cathryn picks up her knitting and gets back to work. Philip does not enter immediately.

CATHRYN

Do you want me to help you? I have always loved to watch you pack.

No sound.

What time did you say your plane is leaving?

No reply.

During the night, of course, like all planes leaving for Europe...

No reply.

I believe it is a very good idea that you go alone. We need a chance to breathe. I have really changed, you know. Before, I would be so anxious every time you had to leave.

Enter Philip, in a splendid mood.

PHILIP

This time, I will tour Paris on foot. No metro, no bus, no taxi. I am going to walk, walk, walk. Nothing but the hustle and bustle of the streets. All the bistros, the cafes and, of course, the Parisians.

CATHRYN

Do go back to that small bistro where we had

88

so much fun. You know, the one with the pin-ball machines, in the Latin Quarter?

PHILIP

The time you won all my money?

CATHRYN

It was the only time we ever played together.

Exit Philip.

Cathryn puts down her knitting for a moment, then picks it up again.

CATHRYN

I too would love to get away, travel all the time, go around the world, like a comet. But women are more like the North Star. Always in place. Oh I am sorry, that was your line.

PHILIP

From the bedroom.

Not about the North Star.

CATHRYN

No, very true. It makes sense that men should be comets. They always have a following: lots and lots of women, children, all sorts of people, changes, crises, telephone wires.

She laughs.

A real nonstop choreography! You know, it gave me an idea for a pas de deux which I started but abandoned. As usual! It is so difficult! What do I do? A pas de deux about two comets? Two comets colliding: bang, an explosion! Two comets traveling side by side? No, that isn't dramatic enough. One comet and the North Star? Too static.

Short pause.

It could be two comets meeting and then separating. Only I hate sad endings. I know I can't be a child forever, but why rush it? The hardest part is to make a pas de deux that fits with the movement of the stars. It's not clear in my mind how it would work. It seems such an enormous task. Can't be a very good idea.

Philip returns, still in a good mood.

PHILIP

Try and imagine one thing: the French, all of them together, discovering one day that freedom of expression in America is one hundred years ahead. The whole country shuts up in shame for two minutes! For two minutes, the decibel volume on the planet goes down two degrees. It is a planetary revolution, the stars have nothing to hold them up, they begin to fall to earth. The moon pivots in one swing. Billions of flies can be heard buzzing around.

Then the French start up again louder than ever. "It's not true," "Oh yes it is," "It's the President's fault" — everything is the President's fault over there.

CATHRYN

Exactly like here.

PHILIP

No, not really.

CATHRYN

What is the difference?

PHILIP

How often have you been to Europe, Cathryn?

CATHRYN

As often as you have taken me, Philip. I never found the French journalists to be more backward than ours.

PHILIP

Aren't you the critic, Cathryn?

Exit Philip.

I am being critical! You are the one putting down the French, not I. You make me laugh!

Short pause. Then sarcastically.

Everyone in the dance group is into free love. You sleep with anybody you want and it doesn't upset your partner. In theory, of course. So everybody intermingles with everybody else and, the next morning, they talk about it in order to 'share' the experience. We are doing this, if you can imagine, not me, but the others, as food for a show we are putting on about the liberated spirit of our generation. Sociologists say we are special. I don't know where they got that idea. I don't have the feeling that our generation sleeps around anymore than yours does... You can imagine the kind of rehearsals we have. People are tense, trying hard to conceal it, yet... Even the smells get all tangled up.

Spotlight on Cathryn who addresses the audience.

For a long time, I was a moth. I wanted to burn my wings in the flame, but I ended up smashing my head against the window pane. Every time. Always. Always. I had a choice: either I would smash up against the window pane or let myself burn in the flame.

Back to regular lighting. Philip enters and takes a seat.

PHILIP

Well, I am through. Great! I have nothing left to do except live. And in Paris! A real vacation! This is what promotions are about, you know. The more you get paid, the less you work. It is simply ridiculous!

CATHRYN

You are exaggerating.

PHILIP

No, I'm not. Everything is unbelievably programmed over there, right up to the etiquette blunders. It is like following a music score. I have the feeling that all my work has been done for me. I will finally be able to enjoy being a free man in town.

CATHRYN

Look, Phil, I know you are not always happy with me. If you think about it a little, you must admit it isn't that bad, truly. I am not ugly and certainly not stupid. I cook well enough, even very well. We entertain friends together and it has even become pleasant,

93

hasn't it? I get along well with the kids. I pay my share of the rent. And I only spend the money that I earn myself. I know I might be too slow for you sometimes, but that is what I call differences of temperament. And I love you. I learn a lot from you. I give you a lot of attention, sometimes too much, sometimes not enough, at least in your opinion, but still and all, I love you. More than I have ever loved anybody in my life. You can't be that miserable, can you? I know you want more than that, but if I knew what it was, I would give it to you. The problem is that I don't know what it is you want nor do I think you do yourself.

PHILIP

Cathryn, you are selling yourself and it is very unpleasant.

CATHRYN

I am not selling myself. I am simply trying to tell you that you could settle down. If you had that home in the country you have been talking about, you could be writing great, powerful articles, perhaps even begin the book you have been wanting to write for years.

PHILIP

I am not ready yet.

CATHRYN

You will never be ready. You will die before you are ready. But I could start looking for a cottage home during your absence.

PHILIP

Cathryn, you will not reorganize my life while I am away.

CATHRYN

You are always saying that is what you want to do. Yet whenever I suggest it, you say no. Perhaps you should get your act together.

PHILIP

What would happen to your career if you lived in the country?

CATHRYN

Shutting herself in.

I never wanted a career and you know it.

PHILIP

That is what you say!

CATHRYN

That is what I say and that is what I know.

PHILIP

Only I have a different version!

CATHRYN

Really?

PHILIP

You always wanted a career, but you never had the courage to admit it. Which is quite different!

CATHRYN

Quite! You seem to know me better than I do. How interesting!

PHILIP

Anyone who is envious of a friend who does three little steps on a stage...!

CATHRYN

Defending herself calmly.

That's just it! It means that those three little insignificant steps are exactly what you don't feel like doing, not even for the sake of a career.

PHILIP

If I had to choose between three little steps

and teaching exercise classes, I would choose the little steps.

CATHRYN

What I teach is not just any kind of exercise.

PHILIP

It still remains only exercise, and not dance.

CATHRYN

Teaching exercise classes is not a disgrace.

PHILIP

It certainly is, in terms of the career you are hoping to build for yourself.

CATHRYN

All you ever think about is career and success. I am not like that.

PHILIP

You are. But you are stiff with fear. Rather than fight for what you want, you complain that others get in your way. Until you can face up to what you want, you will never succeed. If only you had the courage to admit that, there would be one less lie you would have to cope with.

CATHRYN

I will admit anything you want. I don't care.
Just as long as you admit that you can't wait to
get away.

PHILIP

No way! I am not bargaining with you.

CATHRYN

I see. I am asked to admit that I am a failure, a
good-for-nothing, that I am wasting my life,
while you can go on believing your own lies,
pretending that everyone else believes them.

PHILIP

We are talking about you, not about me. But
since you are on the topic, why not admit that
you don't want me to leave.

CATHRYN

What do you mean? I always thought it was
perfectly normal that you travel.

PHILIP

Oh really? Then why is it that just before I
leave you tell me you love me?

CATHRYN

Don't I say the same thing when you come back?

PHILIP

What does it mean?

CATHRYN

That I love you — no?

PHILIP

Very funny... I don't buy that.

CATHRYN

All right! What do you think it means? I know you are going to do me the honor of telling me that you always know exactly what I am thinking about.

PHILIP

It is so obvious, a child could see it. You dread seeing me leave, so much so that you cling to me like a bloodsucker. I have the feeling that I am being trapped in a spider web. And it keeps getting worse and worse. I feel more and more guilty each time I must leave.

CATHRYN

I pity you!

PHILIP

It isn't my fault if you feel abandoned. If you haven't understood the demands of a journalist's life, then you haven't understood a thing.

CATHRYN

I may understand very little, but one thing has become obvious to me in the last six months. Every time you leave, you put me down and use me like a springboard. You imagine that the minute you step out of *here*, you will be happier. You think that once you get *there*, nobody will contradict you — as if I ever contradicted you. You think I don't see how thrilled you are about leaving. When you come back, strange how you don't hold your head up so high. I know you're wondering...

She mimics Philip's voice.

...how come you didn't feel as good as you thought you would...

She stops mimicking him.

You don't feel better *there* than you do *here*. And that, by the way, is no fault of mine. But, of course, this is none of my business.

PHILIP

Then why talk about it? Why keep sticking

your nose in my business? I can't make a move anymore without you watching me. I can't speak without you turning every word against me. I have the right to live without being the subject of a damn thesis. You think living with you is interesting? You think it is a lot of fun?

CATHYRN

Personally, I don't see anything wrong with it.

PHILIP

Don't you see what you've turned into? What are you doing wearing a nightgown at this time of the day?

CATHRYN

What do you mean: what am I doing? I'm cold!

PHILIP

You should see what you look like.

CATHRYN

I look like a woman wearing a nightgown. But I can always take it off if you wish.

PHILIP

To top it off, you are knitting.

CATHRYN

Yes, I am knitting. I can stop if you want me to.

PHILIP

You are doing your best not to understand a thing, aren't you?

CATHRYN

I have always enjoyed knitting. I guess that this isn't a good enough reason. You probably see a hidden meaning which naturally escapes me because I am completely deaf, dumb and blind.

PHILIP

You look like a little housewife waiting for her husband to get back home while the dinner gets cold. A little housewife knitting time away.

CATHRYN

You have a point there: you are often late!

PHILIP

You are more married than a married woman. And what's worse, you are far more arrogant.

CATHRYN

A good thing I turned down your marriage proposal. That must be a relief to you! We would really be in a blind alley by now, wouldn't we?

PHILIP

Go ahead and look down on marriage as much as you want to. You could do worse. Why not try out the free love thing during my absence!

CATHRYN

I am not interested.

PHILIP

Why don't you try sleeping with somebody else? That might get you aroused for a change.

CATHRYN

Why should I sleep with somebody else? Like it or not, my problem is with you, and it is with *you* that I must solve it.

PHILIP

Have you ever once imagined that perhaps I want to know whether or not you have similar problems with other men?

CATHRYN

So you could say that it wasn't your fault! Don't count on it.

PHILIP

Maybe you should stop bartering your ass in return for fidelity as every married woman has been doing since the beginning of time.

CATHRYN

For all the good that has done! If anything, I have been wasting my time.

PHILIP

Oh, get off it, Cathryn, give up. Go give your attention to someone else. Go play the North Star elsewhere.

CATHRYN

She follows the same thread of thought until the end of the scene.

I will admit anything you want, Phil. You're right! Yes, I am housewifey. Yes, I want a career. I want it so badly I drool about it. Yes, I cling to you. No, I don't dance. No, I will never be a good dancer. Yes, I am everything you say I am...

PHILIP

You are jealous!

CATHRYN

Oh, jealous, I had forgotten that one!

PHILIP

Possessive!

CATHRYN

...Possessive? Like hell. How can I be possessive, I only see you three minutes a day and
even then you want to be somewhere else.

PHILIP

Yes, because you are possessive.

CATHRYN

Possessive! Christ! What do I care at this point.
Look: there is only one thing I can't accept
and never will. I know you have a woman
everywhere you go...

PHILIP

That is none of your business.

CATHRYN

Of course, it is none of my business. A

woman's ass is a man's business, but a man's ass is his business and his alone. Of course! "That is how it goes, dear little Cathy. I am going to teach you well how to live your life."

PHILIP

See how you are. You should see your face right now. You should see how ugly you are right now.

CATHRYN

So now, I am ugly! One more thing. Let me say this to you: your ass is my business when I join you in one of those foreign places and I can tell by the way some woman is looking at you that you slept with her before I got there!

PHILIP

If only you knew what a relief it is to be away from your clutches.

CATHRYN

Possibly! So what! That is not what I mean. I can bear those little affairs. I know it is just a question of chance. You arrive some place and you take the first thing you can lay your hands on just as long as it has an ass and a pair of tits.

PHILIP

Can't you see how much you despise women,
how much you despise everybody?

CATHRYN

But what I cannot stand is that you plan your
affairs ahead of time, that you decide who you
are going to fuck on your trips, when and
where. Don't say it isn't true. You should not
leave your post cards hanging around. That, I
can't take. I really cannot. And do you mind
telling me what this relationship means, what
our living together means? Do you mind telling me why I am living with you? It doesn't
make sense anymore.

PHILIP

How can you tell if I am going to fuck somebody else or not? You have never had friends
you were eager to see? Of course not, you
don't have any friends! Not a one! And let me
remind you that you are living with me
because you chose to. Because you wanted to.
And if you don't like it, you can leave. I won't
hold you back, don't worry. But no, you
can't. Instead, you cling, cling, cling to me
like a fucking bloodsucker. You can't live
without me, Cathryn. So just plan your own
life as you please, but let me live mine in
peace.

Exit Philip.

CATHRYN
Screaming.

Philip!

Fade out.

SCENE FIVE

BRILLANTE CON FUOCO

Pride

A year later.

Late evening.

Enter Cathryn, Philip and Valentino. All three have been drinking. Philip rambles on uncontrollably; he seems restless and goaded by a smoldering anger which tapers off towards the middle of the scene. At first, Valentino looks at Philip with admiration, but later on becomes frightened by what is going on. Cathryn is bold but calm, cold and, at certain times, very sharp. When she enters, she opens a bottle of champagne which she begins to pour into three glasses.

PHILIP

Very friendly towards Valentino.

In all the years we have known each other, Valentino, is this really the first time I have invited you over?

VALENTINO

It is only normal. We are from different worlds.

PHILIP

Like hell! You are one of the people I feel most comfortable with. You are my people!

VALENTINO

Ah, that is nice of you.

PHILIP

We often thought of inviting you over. Tell him, Cathy.

CATHRYN

Refusing to lie.

We have? I don't remember.

PHILIP

Come on, just last month again, we talked about it.

CATHRYN

Maybe we did.

PHILIP

To Valentino, obviously starting a game of some sort and trying to get Valentino on his side.

Women, my friend, women! Tell me, you must have had a very thrilling life…

VALENTINO

Not as much as you.

PHILIP

You are too modest, my friend, much too modest! Everybody knows your life has been one conquest after the other…

VALENTINO

I now feel embarrassed.

PHILIP

Have you ever noticed during this exciting life of yours a strange thing which, basically, goes like this: every positive action in the world brings on a negative action which in turn destroys the positive action? It never fails! You see that with couples a lot, especially those who have been together a long time. You know what I am talking about? I am sure you do, you see couples all day long. Isn't there always one half of the couple that says yes, while the other one says no? Always!

VALENTINO

That is very true. It is like night and day, like black and white. When I say yes, my wife says no, and when I say no...

PHILIP

You got it! Yes! For a man's positive action to come to life, bear fruit and *not be destroyed*, you have got to wring the neck of the negative action, literally. Only a cold, calculated decision can save the positive actions of the world. Have you ever noticed that too?

VALENTINO

Ah, you can't be negative, that is for sure...

CATHRYN

Laughing. She moves towards Philip.

Do you want to wring my neck?

VALENTINO

You are funny. He was only joking. I am sure nobody would want to wring the neck of such

112

a pretty woman!

PHILIP

No, Valentino, this young woman is not funny. Those nice, obliging manners of hers are nothing but a front. Underneath that is a nasty temper. That pretty neck of hers, you know, is attached to such a strong backbone that I have never managed, but never managed to bend it, not once. You know what I mean, Valentino?

CATHRYN

You are wrong, Phil. You have bent it all right.

VALENTINO

Trying to be comforting.

Well, look at it this way. It wasn't a waste. It is the kind of thing that keeps the fire going, keeps you young. That is why you are in such fine shape.

PHILIP

That comes from my fighting back, Valentino. That is all it is. You have to be able to resist every kind of attack, whether low or mean or mediocre if you don't want to lose your soul. Did you know she was a witch, Valentino? Did you know she delved into charms and spells? Incantations, she calls them. Do an incantation for us, Cathy. I am sure you could for our friend here who has never seen you dance. Am I wrong, Valentino?

VALENTINO

No, I am sorry, but no, I...

CATHRYN

Don't feel bad, lots of people have never seen me dance.

She laughs.

VALENTINO

But I will go see you. I will, and I am sure I will like it very much.

PHILIP

You had better watch out, Valentino, or you will end up being one of her disciples. You know she has fans who fell in love with her the first time they saw her and went back to see her ten times!

CATHRYN

Laughing.

Oh yes, ten times, at least!

PHILIP

What do you make of that, Valentino?

VALENTINO

Well, Cathryn has a lot of charm and presence...

PHILIP

That isn't the reason. She is a witch, I swear. She has implored some goddess, I don't know which one, and now she has a sort of gift, some strange power. She bewitches whoever she wants. Well, almost! Do a little incantation for us, Cathy. Let's see if we too will become your disciples. Come on, let's see if you can bewitch us!

CATHRYN

But, of course, with pleasure!

> *Cathryn, half-amused, half-tense executes a short series of bizarre and wild exercises which she ends with a ah-ya-hum utterance! She immediately raises her head, smiling.*

So?

PHILIP

Isn't this blowing your mind, Valentino? You are going to become one of her disciples now?

VALENTINO

Turning to Philip.

Well, it is very beautiful. Don't you think it is beautiful, Philip?

PHILIP

You see, you have become a disciple!

CATHRYN

Laughing.

I sure hope not!

VALENTINO

What does ah-ya-hum mean?

CATHRYN

I don't really know. Something like: May your will be done or nothing at all. It depends on the moment, I guess.

PHILIP

May your will be done. Can you just imagine that? From someone who has never obeyed anyone in her life.

CATHRYN

Unaggressively. Playing along in the game.

Maybe I have changed. Why don't you test me?

PHILIP

Stop acting and pour the champagne.

CATHRYN

Prostrating herself saying:

Ah-ya-hum.

She raises her head.

May I please have some too?

PHILIP

No, you have had enough for tonight.

CATHRYN

Prostrating herself, saying:
Ah-ya-hum.

> *She pours champagne for the two men, then goes to sit down without taking any herself.*

PHILIP

What you have just seen, Valentino, was a stunning display of deceit. A true performance. She has danced for you, she has acted for you and she is acting right now for you. It is absolutely wonderful, you have to admit.

VALENTINO

Ah, I see.

To Cathryn who brings him a glass of champagne.

Thank you very much, thank you.

PHILIP

Cathryn brings him a glass of champagne.

You have to be able to distinguish fact from fiction. You think you are seeing nice, obliging behavior. But beware, Valentino, there is a destructive will power at work underneath it all. Can't you feel it, Valentino?

Cathryn sits down without taking any champagne. Valentino becomes increasingly uncomfortable.

PHILIP

Let's drink, my friend, let's drink to our health!

VALENTINO

Oh, but aren't you going to have a drink? Here, let me get a glass for you.

CATHRYN

No, Valentino. He said *no*. So be it!

VALENTINO

I can't drink by myself in the company of a pretty woman. It simply isn't done...

PHILIP

On the contrary! It is done. For once in her life she obeys. Let's take advantage of it. You don't know how unusual it is.

VALENTINO

That isn't very gentlemanly.

Valentino goes towards Cathryn, but Philip stops him.

PHILIP

Stop, Valentino. Don't be fooled by appearances. She is trying to break us up you and me, can't you see? If you take pity on her, that's it for us, the game is over.

VALENTINO

Please, tell me what to do? I don't know what to do anymore.

PHILIP

Sit down. I will explain everything to you. You really think she is obeying me right now?

VALENTINO

That is what you said just a moment ago.

Cathryn bursts out laughing.

Isn't it true?

PHILIP

I was joking! The truth is: she isn't. She does all that to drag you over to her side, do you understand? If you side with her, you are against me and the war is on. That is what war is all about. The psychological war, the war of nerves. Cathryn's very good at that!

VALENTINO

I only want her to have a drink.

PHILIP

She has never obeyed, Valentino, never. She is like those slaves who think they can become stronger than their master. They remain slaves all their lives but boss the master around. Admit that you think you're stronger than me, Cathryn, come on.

CATHRYN

Prostrating herself.

I think that you think that I am stronger than you.

PHILIP

Repeat *exactly* what I said!

CATHRYN

You think that I think that I am stronger than you.

PHILIP

To Valentino.

Do you see what I mean, Valentino? She does exactly what she wants and nothing else. It may seem as if I were dominating her, but, in reality, she is the one who dominates me. Otherwise, I would have told her to disappear a long time ago.

CATHRYN

Prostrating herself and rolling on the floor. Repeating:

Ah-ya-hum.

PHILIP

I have seen better disappearing acts, Cathryn! Consider yourself lucky, Valentino. She has given us two performances in one evening.

VALENTINO

Come on. Please sit down.

PHILIP

You see, Valentino, you can always complain that your wife is forever telling you what to do, that she talks too much...

VALENTINO

Ah no, no, no. That isn't what I really meant!

PHILIP

But your wife, I am sure, is a real woman. I am sure she takes good care of you, your house, your children.

VALENTINO

Ah yes, she does, and very well in fact.

PHILIP

If only Cathryn would tell me what to do once in a while. I would love to be able to lean on her. But this woman is a dancer now, she doesn't do anything around here anymore. Nothing, I tell you. Coming home now is like walking into a dump. Look, nothing has been dusted around here since I don't know when. When are you going to come home and dust the furniture, Cathryn?

CATHRYN

She cannot believe what she has heard.

What? Dust? Dust what for Christ's sake?

PHILIP

The furniture. Everything! I want you to dust everything, right now!

CATHRYN

Starting to laugh.

Right now? What is the occasion?

PHILIP

To Valentino.

See how well she obeys, Valentino!

To Cathryn.

Everything is dusty, that is why. There is so much dust, you can't see what is beneath it. Your house is one big dump, Cathryn. It is buried in dust, piled up high with garbage!

CATHRYN

I must remember to tell the cleaning lady to dust next time.

PHILIP

I don't want the cleaning lady to do it, I want you to do it. I want you to become responsible for your house. I want you to do what you have to do, to do everything you have to do.

Including dusting, do you hear me?

CATHRYN

Yes, you are certainly speaking loud enough!

Her actions match her words.

Look, Phil, I can do anything. In fact, I am doing anything. I can get on all fours. Look: I am on all fours. I can crawl at your feet, lick your toes, climb up your legs, kiss you all over, take off your shirt...

PHILIP

Embarrassed, not knowing whether to be proud or amused.

Stop that monkey business, will you.

CATHRYN

Still glued to him.

All right. But I won't dust the house, it is ridiculous!

PHILIP

Lifting and shaking her.

Oh, but you will, do you hear me? You will do exactly what I tell you to do!

CATHRYN

Firmly.

Never! It is too ridiculous!

PHILIP

Oh but you will. You will or I will...

CATHRYN

You will what? Strangle me?

PHILIP

Powerless and uncontrollably angry.

Will you ever give in?

CATHRYN

No.

PHILIP

Will you ever get tired of saying *no*?

CATHRYN

No.

PHILIP

Goddam, give in Cathryn.

CATHRYN

Freeing herself.

Never. Let me go.

PHILIP

Didn't I tell you, Valentino. This woman is a bundle of lies.

Philip has let go of Cathryn. Valentino rises; he is extremely uncomfortable.

VALENTINO

I... I thank you for everything, I... but I really must be going.

PHILIP

Come on, my friend... Aren't you staying to finish the bottle?

VALENTINO

I have to get up early tomorrow, I have to work and...

PHILIP

Tomorrow is Sunday. You don't work on Sundays.

VALENTINO

Ah, but I have work to do at home and the children, they get up early and everything...

CATHRYN

Go, Valentino, go, the evening has come to an end...

PHILIP

Are you throwing my friend out now?

VALENTINO

Defensive.

No, no. I was about to leave...

CATHRYN

Forget it, Valentino. Thanks anyway.

VALENTINO

Good night... er... good morning!

Valentino leaves as quickly as he can. Short pause.

PHILIP

Turning to Cathryn aggressively.

Since when do you throw my friends out?

127

CATHRYN

Exhausted.

Philip, stop it.

PHILIP

Before I met you, my house used to be full of laughter, full of action. You have isolated me from everything and everybody I loved. You can be proud of yourself!

CATHRYN

No, Philip. You have done that yourself. You didn't need my help.

PHILIP

Oh yeah? And what about my children? Who turned them against me if it wasn't you?

CATHRYN

If you weren't always telling them how to live their lives, maybe they would come and see you more often. And stop strangling that glass, you will break it!

PHILIP

I will do what I please; this is my home. That is all I have left, so I will break as many glasses as I want in my own house!

He breaks his glass.

CATHRYN

Anybody can break glasses. You don't even have to be smart to do that. It is easy. Look.

She calmly drops her glass on the floor.

PHILIP

You are completely crazy. You are hysterical! You need a psychiatrist, do you know that?

CATHRYN

And I am not even mad!

PHILIP

Pick it up!

CATHRYN

But of course!

Cathryn is about to leave.

PHILIP

Come back here.

CATHRYN

Coming back.

Stop it, Phil. You are not destroying me, you are destroying yourself.

PHILIP

It is your pride that has to be broken down. That habit of yours of wanting to be right all the time! You can be proud of what you have accomplished, Cathryn. You are a dancer now! Only you think you have gotten some place when all you wanted out of life was to move your feet and your arms at the same time and show everybody how good you were. Everybody thinks you are a little genius, but don't worry, it won't last. Because your triumph is a worthless triumph for a worthless project.

CATHRYN

For five years, you told me to go ahead and dance. Now that I am a dancer, you tell me to stay home. For five years, you told me to stand on my feet. Now that I do stand on my feet, you want me to crawl again. Make up your goddam mind, Philip.

PHILIP

You are right, Cathryn. You are always right! One day, you are going to find yourself alone, Miss Right, with your self-righteousness. The crowd is always ready to call anybody a genius. But sooner or later, it comes up with another so-called genius, someone younger, crazier, more beautiful. You will see, you will end up completely alone, Cathryn, with your self-righteousness.

CATHRYN

Maybe.

Exit Cathryn.

PHILIP

Where are you going?

CATHRYN

To get the broom and the dustpan.

PHILIP

Calling after her.

People like you should be swept off the planet. You don't believe in anything, you laugh at everything that has any value. You destroy everything. You have taken everything I had, everything. I used to be a happy man, I was active, I loved what I was doing and I knew why I was doing it. There was a certain order in my life and, oddly enough, a happy disorder as well. I used to put my whole heart into living. Now, I have got nothing left, nothing.

CATHRYN

She comes back a moment later with a broom and a dustpan to pick up the pieces of broken glass.

You are not a man, Philip. You are a journalist.

PHILIP

What is that supposed to mean?

CATHRYN

You want to change the world. You can't even fix yourself a cup of coffee calmly. You can't bear to hear the speeches you have been hearing for fifteen years, still you want more speeches. Because you don't know anything else. You are desperately unhappy but you don't even make an effort to change. You fight me because I am not as unhappy as you are. And you can't stand that! You only live for your work. You have never been interested in anything else. Never. You are a great journalist, Philip, but so what!

PHILIP

You have taken all I had. I have nothing left, not even respect for my work. Leave. I am fed up with your love. Go give it to somebody else, if anybody wants it, of course... Personally, I can't stand it anymore.

Cathryn is on the floor. She cries softly during the following speech.

CATHRYN

Short pause.

You told me once I had never given you flowers. You were right, I hadn't. I had never even thought about it. I wasn't very demonstrative. The next day, I bought you some flowers, but it was too late. You didn't believe it was spontaneous. You were right. It was always like that. I tried to make you happy. God, did I ever! I was clumsy, I know. I wasn't what you call 'sensitive'. And then my love became a burden. I wasn't much fun to sleep with. And then, and then, and then... Everything you say is true. Except I didn't take everything away from you. I am not the one who drove everybody away from you. You did that all by yourself. You sent all your friends away, one after the other. One night or the other. I am the only one left. I wouldn't mind staying, I swear, I would stay. But there is nothing I can do, nothing at all. Whether I hate you or love you with all my heart makes no difference. That is what is so terrible. I can't keep watching you fight so blindly and struggle like you were possessed. I can't stand to see you fight me all the time. I don't ask much of you anymore, that is what hurts the most. I don't have anything left either, Philip.

I have lost what I loved most in the world: you. And all I can do is leave you like everybody else.

PHILIP

I don't know what to live for anymore, Cathryn.

CATHRYN

Nor do I.

She gets to her feet.

PHILIP

Screaming and extending his arms to her.

Cathryn!

Lights change.
Cathryn turns to the audience.

CATHRYN

One day, towards the end, I made a list of everything I wanted Philip to be. It was a long list, a very long list. And not one bit like him. So I laughed and tore it up. We shouldn't ask more of people than we would of dogs — just to be themselves, that is all. Later, I decided to stay with him till the bitter end. Till the last barrier was crossed. To go to the end, to consummate something at least once in my life. It was then I realized that only when you've lost everything, everything becomes possible.

Fade out.

SCENE SIX

GRAVE

Tenderness

A year later.

The doorway of a small restaurant.

Cathryn and Philip have just finished lunch and are getting ready to leave. They are greatly affected at having seen each other and they laugh nervously without apparent reason to conceal a certain shyness. While their discussion brings out some of their old habits, they nevertheless look at each other with warm consideration.

Valentino brings Cathryn's coat.

VALENTINO

Good day, Miss.

CATHRYN

Thank you, Valentino. It was delicious.

VALENTINO

The pleasure was all mine.

PHILIP

So long, Valentino. See you soon.

VALENTINO

Politely.

Of course, Sir. *Ciao!*

*Valentino walks away. Cathryn and Philip
leave the restaurant. Philip looks around.*

PHILIP

What a nice day!

CATHRYN

I am glad you are not in a hurry.

PHILIP

Yes! Well, even though I am working hard, I
still have some time for myself.

CATHRYN

Thank you for calling, Philip. I don't think I would have had the courage to phone you myself.

PHILIP

Why not?

CATHRYN

I didn't know how you were doing. I watched you come back into the public eye... but I didn't know if you were under a lot of pressure or...

PHILIP

Well, as you can see, I am taking the pressure very well. I have vented my rage by writing two hundred pages of seething useless stuff and now I feel relieved.

CATHRYN

You are not going to write anymore?

PHILIP

I don't know. If I ever write again, it will not be in seclusion. I need action around me. You know I am not a hermit. There is no demand for my kind of writing, so I can take my time. I don't take myself for a messiah anymore either, so I can write what I really want. You see I am learning how to wait for things to take shape a little. Besides, it isn't what you say that counts, but how you say it, don't you think?

CATHRYN

Maybe. Guess what, I started choreographing complete pieces. With a beginning, a middle and an end.

PHILIP

Are you going to stop dancing?

CATHRYN

No, not dancing, just performing.

PHILIP

Why? How can you become famous if you don't perform?

CATHRYN

It doesn't really matter. I don't like doing one-woman shows.

PHILIP

You are so strange!

CATHRYN

Well, that is how I am.

PHILIP

I had almost forgotten what you were like.
Not that I know now, for that matter.

Short pause. Making fun of himself.

Do you know what? I still want to get married.

CATHRYN

Still?

PHILIP

Hm, hm! Every time I start over, I feel like
getting married. However this time I want a
small simple wedding and only two children,
not ten. See how reasonable I have become.

CATHRYN

Very impressive! Have you found someone?

PHILIP

I thought of you at first…

CATHRYN

Oh my God!

PHILIP

You mean you would have turned me down?

CATHRYN

You bet!

PHILIP

Phew, what a relief!

CATHRYN

You said it!

PHILIP

You see, we have developed good common habits. We are used to each other's way of fighting among other things...

CATHRYN

That is just it!

PHILIP

After thinking it over, I decided I should make an effort to try and find someone else. I thought you probably had your share of fighting which, of course, is not without great merit on your part.

CATHRYN

Thanks. Yes, starting over and dragging along old habits can't be too much fun!

PHILIP

That is exactly what I told myself. See how well we are getting along.

CATHRYN

Couldn't be better!

They laugh a little. A short silence.

CATHRYN

No kidding, do you still want to get married?

PHILIP

I may not go that far, but do you know of anything else that is worth doing?

CATHRYN

Anything else worth doing…? I don't know. I don't have such a hard time doing things anymore. Most of the time now, I just do them without thinking.

PHILIP

Are you trying to say that you don't look any farther than the tip of your nose?

CATHRYN

Phil, no matter how hard we try, I don't think we can find any real reasons for living. Maybe it is because there are too many, that is just it.

PHILIP

My God, you have become a philosopher!

CATHRYN

I always was, I think. It just didn't show.

PHILIP

Cathryn, watch it. You are burying your head in the sand. I am still searching, at least. I keep getting bumps on my head from banging it on the wall so much, but I haven't given up, I just keep searching!

CATHRYN

You didn't get hurt enough yet?

PHILIP

I am good at nursing myself, thank you.

CATHRYN

I am sorry. It is really none of my business, but I think it is possible to search quietly, you know.

PHILIP

Maybe, I don't know. You are probably right.

CATHRYN

God! I don't want to be right all the time. I
don't want that to be my reason for living.

PHILIP

Well, well, what do you know! So when you
said you didn't have any...

CATHRYN

... I wasn't telling the whole truth. What a
drag! Nobody really changes, do they?

Short pause.

PHILIP

Well, I have to go now.

CATHRYN

I understand.

They take a few steps.

PHILIP

I wanted to tell you. Over there in my secluded
country house, I have been practicing making
my coffee calmly, but I still can't do it. The

only thing I do calmly is sleep.

They laugh.

I do keep trying, you know! Well, I guess…

They hesitate.

CATHRYN

Thank you, Philip.

PHILIP

For what?

CATHRYN

For the lunch, for everything.

PHILIP

Please. It was my pleasure.

CATHRYN

I don't know why you wanted to see me, but I am glad you did.

PHILIP

Me too. You have changed, you know.

CATHRYN

So have you.

They hesitate again.

CATHRYN

I wish you would take me in your arms.

They hug each other. They are very moved.

CATHRYN

God, this feels good!

PHILIP

What we had together wasn't all that bad, was it?

CATHRYN

It was very good. We had good fights, you and I.

They go in different directions.

Valentino moves forward.

VALENTINO

Love is not such a big deal after all! It passes away. The only thing that lasts is the family. They don't talk about that in the papers, though. They'd rather talk about tragic love stories. Personaly, I don't care for tragic love stories anymore, so, I don't read the papers. Things like that are not going to happen to me anyway. So tell me, why should I bother.

The lights fade on the stage.

THE END

Printed by
the workers of
Ateliers Graphiques Marc Veilleux Inc.
Cap-Saint-Ignace, Qué.